W9-CMF-813

Parent's Introduction

Whether your child is a beginning reader, a reluctant reader, or an eager reader, this book offers a fun and easy way to encourage and help your child in reading.

Developed with reading education specialists, *We Both Read* books invite you and your child to take turns reading aloud. You read the left-hand pages of the book, and your child reads the right-hand pages—which have been written at one of six early reading levels. The result is a wonderful new reading experience and faster reading development!

You may find it helpful to read the entire book aloud yourself the first time, then invite your child to participate the second time. As you read, try to make the story come alive by reading with expression. This will help to model good fluency. It will also be helpful to stop at various points to discuss what you are reading. This will help increase your child's understanding of what is being read.

In some books, a few challenging words are introduced in the parent's text, distinguished with **bold** lettering. Pointing out and discussing these words can help to build your child's reading vocabulary. If your child is a beginning reader, it may be helpful to run a finger under the text as each of you reads. Please also notice that a "talking parent" ☉ icon precedes the parent's text, and a "talking child" ☉ icon precedes the child's text.

If your child struggles with a word, you can encourage "sounding it out," but keep in mind that not all words can be sounded out. Your child might pick up clues about a word from the picture, other words in the sentence, or any rhyming patterns. If your child struggles with a word for more than five seconds, it is usually best to simply say the word.

Most of all, remember to praise your child's efforts and keep the reading fun. After you have finished the book, ask a few questions and discuss what you have read together. Rereading this book multiple times may also be helpful for your child.

Try to keep the tips above in mind as you read together, but don't worry about doing everything right. Simply sharing the enjoyment of reading together will increase your child's reading skills and help to start your child off on a lifetime of reading enjoyment!

The Mouse in My House
We Both Read® Book

We Both Read® is a trademark of Treasure Bay, Inc.

Published by
Treasure Bay, Inc.
P.O. Box 119
Novato, CA 94948 USA

Printed in Singapore

Library of Congress Control Number: 2011935123

Hardcover ISBN: 978-1-60115-257-2
Paperback ISBN: 978-1-60115-258-9

We Both Read® Books
Patent No. 5,957,693

Visit us online at:
www.webothread.com

PR 11-11

WE BOTH READ®

The Mouse in My House

By Paul Orshoski

Illustrated by Jeffery Ebbeler

TREASURE BAY

Once there was a **tiny mouse**
that made its way inside my house.
And from its tiny little nest . . .

the **tiny mouse** was
one big pest.

3

The mouse would race across my toes.
It liked to chew on all my clothes.
It liked to hide. It came and went, . . .

and with my shirt
it made a tent.

It frightened dad. He threw a mop.
The mouse got dad to blow his top.
It startled mom. She danced a jig.

The mouse made mother flip her wig.

Mom tossed a skate. Dad froze in place.
And that's when Kitty joined the chase.
As Kitty Cat searched on with me, . . .

the mouse just hid
and had hot tea.

While Kitty made a great big fuss,
the mouse just sat and laughed at us.
It popped a hatch and left its cave.

It swung up high
and gave a wave.

Mom saw the mouse and threw a can.
Dad dropped his cup and tossed a pan.
They filled the floor with pads of glue.

They stuck on dad—
and mother too.

The mouse ran swiftly up the sink.
It gave a smirk and then a wink.
The mouse sprayed Kitty with a hose.

This gave the cat
a big wet nose.

While Kitty tucked her tail in tears,
the mouse just grinned from ear to ear.
As Kitty cried, I hatched a plan.

I spun around
and off I ran.

I grabbed some cheese. I set a trap.
And when I heard the mouse trap snap,
I heard a howl. I heard a wail.

I got no mouse—
just Kitty's tail.

We chased the mouse beneath a chair.
But when Dad looked, it was not there.
I tried to trap it in a bowl.

The mouse ran back
into its hole.

As Mom was resting unaware,
the mouse was nibbling on a pear.
It spit the seeds inside Mom's sock.

And then the mouse
ran up the clock.

We trapped it in a corner spot.
The mouse tied Kitty up in knots.
It bopped me on my big old head.

It rang the chime
and then it fled.

Down the stairway near the den,
the mouse was on the loose again.
I jumped the rail and leaped out far . . .

and got the mouse
inside a jar.

We all hopped in my father's truck.
And now the mouse was one sad duck.
We drove as far as one could see, . . .

and then we let the
mouse go free.

The mouse made friends with other mice.
The country mice were really nice.
They ran all night and slept all day.

They liked to dance.
They liked to play.

At first the mouse was glad to roam,
but soon enough it missed our home.
So with some friends it hit the road, . . .

and on a tractor
they all rode.

They slipped inside a **farmer**'s shed.
They had a feast and went to bed.
The cows and chickens gave a shout.

The **farmer** came
and ran them out.

They hopped a train. They rode a bus.
They asked for help from Mailman Gus.
He checked his map. He scratched his ear, . . .

and then Gus led
them back to here.

There were a hundred, maybe more,
when all those mice ran through the door.
They dashed and darted up the wall, . . .

and then the mice
ran down the hall.

We chased them morning, noon, and night.
We would not quit without a fight!
They locked us out and we were beat, . . .

and so we moved across the street.

If you liked *The Mouse in My House,* here is another
We Both Read® Book you are sure to enjoy!

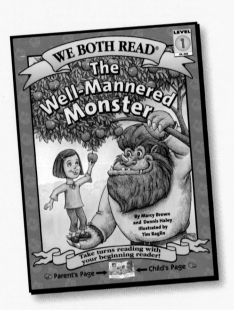

The Well-Mannered Monster

Matt may be a huge, hairy, green monster, but he is the nicest and best-mannered monster you will ever meet. Join Matt and his best friend, Pat, as they help Pat's mom get ready for a big dinner party. The dinner party guests don't know there will be a monster at the party, but Matt is so nice that hopefully everyone will like him and the party will go smoothly.

To see all the We Both Read books that are available,
just go online to **www.WeBothRead.com**